One Day I Picked An Apple

SANDRA L BARNETT

In memory of Carroll Larabee,
and to Nadine Larabee,
who both enabled me to have MANY pets,
including some "farm animals"
that became pets.
Thanks Dad and Mom!

It is a mud-to-the-top-of-my-boots rainy day.

A cold raindrop hits my nose, and I pull my hood tighter
as I dream of warm summer sunshine.

Dreaming of picking
sweet, juicy apples.
Yummmm....

But apple picking
season is months away!
It's springtime now,
lambing season on our
farm.

Warm wooly mama sheep keep their lambs close.
Always watching, always protecting.

They really love their lambs, and so do I.
A pet lamb is what I want!

My mom says, "Oh Lou, sheep are farm animals not pets."
But I think a lamb would be the best pet ever!

The mama sheep watch
and protect their lambs.

In the pasture I hear a strange sound.
I listen....
"Baaa-baaaaa."
A tiny bleat.

Something isn't right.... I look closer.

At the edge of the flock,
I see one small lamb,
all alone.
No mama watching. No mama protecting.

Where is her mama?

The lamb looks for her mother,
but the sheep push her away.

I pick her up and wrap her inside my coat.

My dad once told me lambs who
can't find their mamas are called
bummer lambs.

I hope this lamb is a bummer lamb.

"May I keep her?"

"Did you look for her mother, Lou?" Dad gently asks.
"I know you want a pet lamb,
but is a mama sheep missing her baby?"

I don't want to look for her mother!
I want this lamb to be MY bummer lamb!

I carry her back to the flock and hold her low.
"Whose baby is this?"

Not one sheep claims this lamb!

She's mine!
She snuggles close
to me in my coat,
and I name her Apple.

"Raising a bummer lamb is a big responsibility," Dad says.

He helps me make a cozy place for Apple.

Mom shows me how
to prepare milk for her.

1. Measure milk powder

2. Measure warm water

3. Mix powder with water

4. Pour into bottle

It is milk, but it isn't sheep milk.

Will she drink it?

Sniff

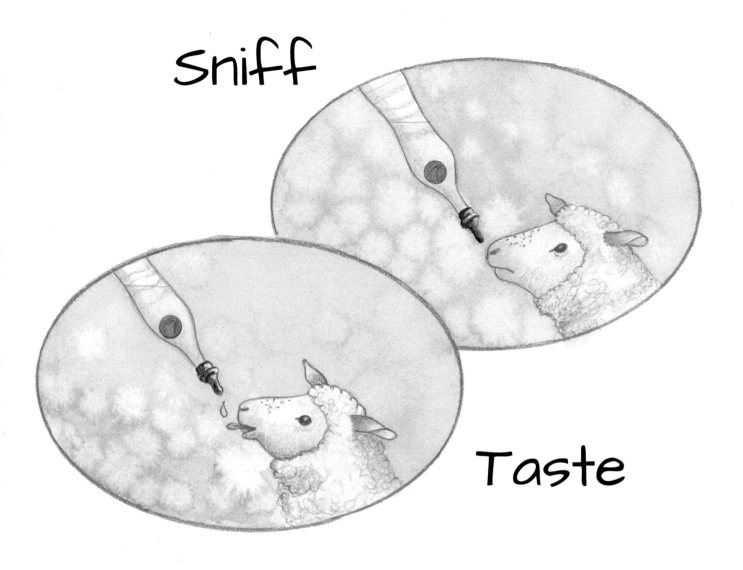

Taste

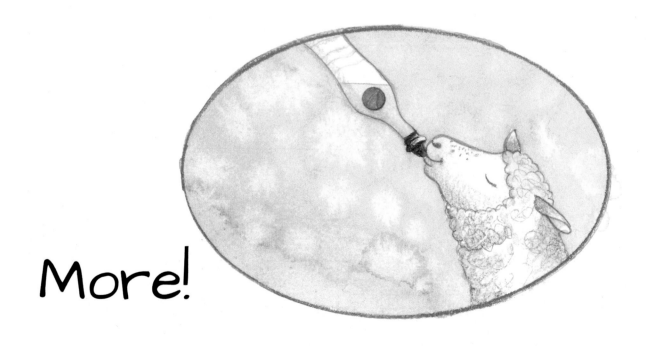

More!

I know she means "Thank you!"

I need to feed Apple two times a day

and once at Midnight.

It's dark! I'm a little bit scared...

and so, so sleepy.

I feed Apple day and night.

She grows and
won't stay in her pen.

Apple wants to play.

Warmer days come.
Apple eats grass and no longer needs milk.
"This lamb is a farm animal, Lou," Dad says.
"Don't you think she is ready to join the
flock and learn sheep ways?"

My heart pounds.

Will I lose my pet?

The next morning
I put Apple with the
flock of sheep.

All day at school, my
tummy feels jumpy.
I can't eat my lunch.

Apple has LAMB FRIENDS!

Has Apple forgotten me?

I remember that mud-to-the-top-of-my-boots rainy day
and know I picked the best kind of apple that day,
my warm, wooly best pet ever....... Apple!

Turn the page for
more information
on bummer lambs
plus
sheep drawing
activity pages

The Real
Apple

Apple came running whenever I called her.
She followed me around the pasture whether
it was raining and snowing
or hot and sunny.
My brother held Apple still so I could get a picture.

More Bummer Lamb Information

When a female sheep, called a ewe, gives birth to a lamb that she can not take care of, that lamb is called a "bummer lamb."
This can happen for the following reasons:

1. A ewe may have twins or triplets and doesn't have enough milk for all of her lambs, so the smallest one gets pushed away.
2. The ewe may be too old or too sick to have enough milk to support even one lamb.
3. Sometimes a lamb gets separated from its mother and they can't find each other.

People can raise bummer lambs to be healthy, productive sheep by regular care and feedings. When the lamb is strong and independent enough, it can join the flock.

M5 RANCH SCHOOL — FIVE MARYS FARMS
www.fivemarysfarms.com/m5-ranch-school
A curriculum for learning by Five Marys Farms.
Learn age-old skills, modern day lessons, animal husbandry, ranch life, outdoor living...
Lessons and workshops on many farm related topics including
All About Sheep and Lambs and *Chores and Caretaking*

How to Bottle Feed a Baby Lamb
Co-authored by Pippa Elliott, MRCVS
https://www.wikihow.com/Bottle-Feed-a-Baby-Lamb
Sometimes, you might need to bottle feed a baby lamb.
Lambs may be orphaned if the mother dies in birth or...

How to Raise an Orphaned Lamb
Co-authored by Ryan Corrigan, LVT, VTS-EVN
https://www.wikihow.com/Raise-an-Orphaned-Lamb
Raising an orphaned lamb can be a fun learning experience...
However, it is also a lot of responsibility...

You can draw sheep. Here are the shapes you need.

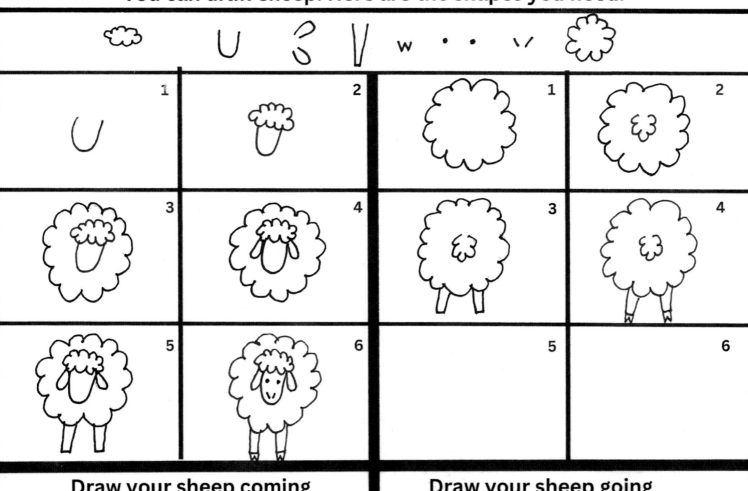

Draw your sheep coming

Draw your sheep going

Draw more sheep

Hello   **Goodbye**

Draw a barn and farm things

Barn		Fences, trees, other ideas	

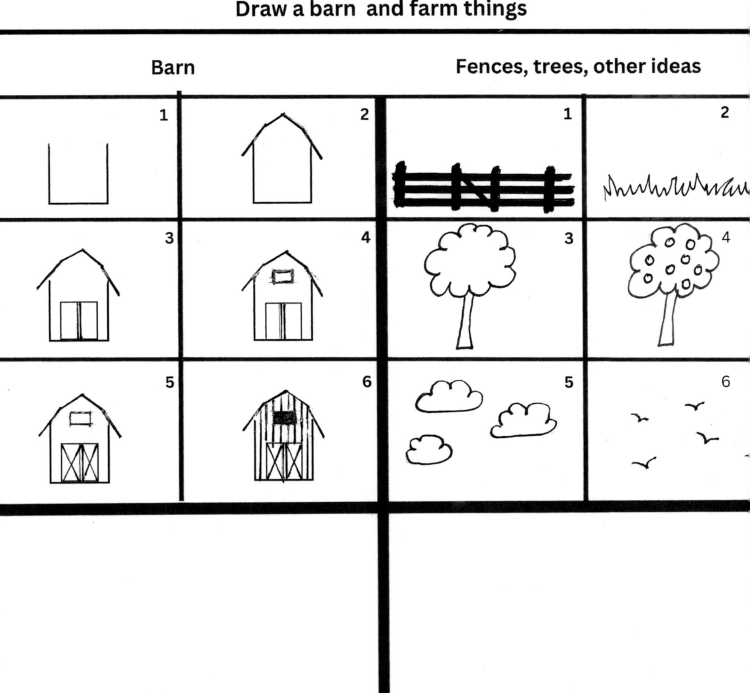

Draw your own sheep farm

Sandra L. Barnett grew up on a small farm in Oregon's Willamette Valley where she had many pets. Some of those pets may have been "farm animals" at one time.

Art has always been Sandra's favorite subject. Homeschooling her own children and later working in a special needs classroom, she enjoyed planning and creating many art projects with the children.

www.SandraLBarnett.com

Made in the USA
Las Vegas, NV
19 September 2023

77530199R00029